Next Please

Ernst Jandl and Norman Junge

NEXT PLEASE
A RED FOX BOOK 0 09 943933 6

First published in Great Britain by Hutchinson,
an imprint of Random House Children's Books

Hutchinson edition published 2001
Red Fox edition published 2003

3 5 7 9 10 8 6 4 2

Red Fox Books are published by Random House Children's Books,
61–63 Uxbridge Road, London W5 5SA,
a division of The Random House Group Ltd,
in Australia by Random House Australia (Pty) Ltd,
20 Alfred Street, Milsons Point, Sydney, NSW 2061, Australia,
in New Zealand by Random House New Zealand Ltd,
18 Poland Road, Glenfield, Auckland 10, New Zealand,
and in South Africa by Random House (Pty) Ltd,
Endulini, 5A Jubilee Road, Parktown 2193, South Africa

THE RANDOM HOUSE GROUP Limited Reg. No. 954009
www.kidsatrandomhouse.co.uk

A CIP catalogue record for this book is available from the British Library.

Printed in Hong Kong

Next Please

Ernst Jandl and Norman Junge

RED FOX

Five are waiting.

Door opens.
One comes out.

"Next, please."
One goes in.

Four waiting.

Door opens.
One comes out.

"Next, please."
One goes in.

Three waiting.

Door opens.
One comes out.

"Next, please."
One goes in.

Two waiting.

Door opens.
One comes out.

"Next, please."
One goes in.

One waiting.
All alone.

Door opens.
One comes out.

"Next, please."
Last one goes in.

"Hello, young fellow, are you the last one?"
"Yes, Doctor. None waiting."

More picture books for you to enjoy:

WHERE THE WILD THINGS ARE
by Maurice Sendak

HAPPY!
by Caroline Castle and Sam Childs

SLOW LORIS
by Alexis Deacon

EGG DROP
by Mini Grey

SQUEAKY CLEAN
by Simon Puttock and Mary McQuillan

BLUE HORSE AND TILLY
by Helen Stephens